Cover design by Spiffing Publishing Ltd

Published by Celestina Press
Paperback ISBN: 978-1-0686301-2-5
eBook ISBN: 978-1-0686301-3-2

CAT BISKIT DAVY

And the Secret Society of Cats

KITTY O'NEILL

Chapter One

The Ancient Tradition of Smuggling

Cat Biskit Davy was my cousin. Well, not exactly my cousin. He *lived* with my distant cousin whose home was one of the old stone houses above the beach in Half Moon Bay at Land's End – the last narrow piece of land which is Cornwall – the south westerly tip of England before the vast open sea stretches out forever.

My ancestors lived in this fishing village for five centuries until they moved to Hampstead, London, in the nineteenth century. They were hoping to find domestic work after huge changes affected the fishing and farming communities. A succession of crop failures and poor harvests caused a lack of food and, in these earlier centuries, being involved in smuggling was a necessary means to eat and stay alive.

Cornwall is famous for smugglers and pirates because the many beaches around its spectacular coastline are secreted by tiny rocky bays, making it easy for ships and boats to sail right into the shoreline unseen. In the dead of night the crew could never be sure if they were approaching the intended official destination to safely make their delivery.

Without moonlight, the beaches would be pitch-black and the arrival dangerous due to jagged rocks invisible beneath the sea's surface. Ships were tricked into sailing into the wrong cove by gangs known as 'wreckers'; they would rob them as the vessel broke into pieces, spilling their treasures. This happened to innocent ships with no connection to organised smuggling, merely aiming to get into a local harbour, unload their cargo for payment, rest for a night and get back out to sea.

If the ship was brought into a beach encircled by houses, the inhabitants would hear the commotion of the wooden ship breaking up. They would often rush down to help themselves and fight over the spilled cargo.

Smugglers have always existed, either as sailors bringing expensive stolen goods into the country or by land distribution without paying government taxes. These consisted of brandy, whisky, wine, tobacco, gold, silver, diamonds and jewels, expensive silk fabrics, exotic spices and wool which carried a high tax. Wool was highly sought after in the rest of Europe. Anything they could secretly sell on to someone else to make money was the target of highly organised networking groups of fifty to one hundred people. The coast's smugglers secretly worked with pirates who robbed ships carrying a valuable haul, either having left England or returning from faraway countries.

Some worked with ships' crews, the deed carried out as the captain slept, unaware they were throwing barrels over the side to float for the smugglers. They rowed out to fetch them in their fishing boats after the ship had silently departed. This was the peaceful scenario.

The more treacherous method of 'wrecking' was deliberately causing a shipwreck. The wreckers shone lanterns or flaming torches from the high clifftops or lit a bonfire on the beach. They signalled to sailors their route into a harbour was safe while they sneakily guided them into an empty, dangerous, deserted place in the eerie darkness. The ship had no chance of arriving in one piece – both cargo and crew tumbling into deep water – making the sailors not only defenceless but likely to drown even before an attack.

With an almighty *crack!* the bottom of the

ship hit the rocks under the waves, splintering the vessel into fragments. The smugglers waiting on the beach rowed out to grab anything afloat. If the sailors who'd fallen into the sea survived, the smugglers frequently killed them to make sure they got their loot – the dead can tell no tales with no one left to recognise and report them.

The smugglers rolled the barrels – some with brandy, wine or glistening treasure – directly through narrow secret tunnels from the beaches into the cellars of nearby houses. All this without being seen or caught transporting by road.

Sometimes hidden trap doors in floorboards, often right under the family's dining table, led down a staircase to the cellar. An escape route reaching another property was usually through a second wiggly tunnel. This precaution meant their haul could be speedily moved on while stalling any police constables or uniformed tax inspectors thumping on the front door.

Since tin mining was an ancient industry in Cornwall it is said that some of the expertly intricate tunnels were dug by tin miners. The passages were low and narrow, barely high enough to run along unless the men were quite short and did not suffer from claustrophobia. Some tunnels could stretch more than a

mile from one village to another. A common route for excavation was from a beach to a nearby inn or tavern.

The nocturnal activity of the smugglers arriving to take away their contraband was masked by the routinely chatty comings and goings of the locals drinking at these busy public houses, today known simply as 'pubs'. The homes with underground passages might be owned by an important person in the village. No one would suspect a doctor or a judge. The nosey characters likely to inform the authorities would not suspect them, least of all the customs inspectors riding about on horseback keeping watch, but very often involved, too. Few would be brave enough to report a doctor without looking foolish, and later finding themselves ill and unable to call for his help. Many desperate people had no other means of putting food on the table and, despite the threat of such severe consequences, continued smuggling as their way of life. The punishment for unpaid taxes or if caught stealing goods was often a prison sentence, perhaps for the rest of their lives in a faraway country on the other side of the world, never to see their families again.

For smuggling and shipwrecking, the punishment could be even worse. As was said in the day, 'they could swing for it' meaning being hung by the neck at a public execution. These were an excuse for jolly outdoor family outings attended by hundreds. Everybody dressed in their best clothes to witness a hanging, bringing with them their small children and even a picnic. The spectators drank so much alcohol that the expression 'to have a hangover' actually came from the headache suffered the morning after a sociable public hanging. If these rowdy crowds were in luck, several alleged criminals might be hung on the same day, to add to their excitement.

Chapter Two

The Arrival

Cat Biskit Davy woke at dawn in a box of wet maps in a puddle in a small sandy cove. He was shipwrecked. There was no sign of his Pirate Queen, Arabella, nor any of his other crew members. He was hungry and quickly found his way towards the old cottages, prowling from house to house, helping himself to other people's food. This was a time many villagers, due to either lack of work and money, were practically starving, but his methods for survival ensured that he was not one of them.

As his name might suggest, Cat Biskit Davy was a cat with a particular weakness. The weakness being biscuits. He had simply become addicted to the type that sailors ate on the ship. In this fishing village they were made and supplied by Mr Duff, the baker. Almost every household kept a supply of ships' biscuits in case they ran out of bread. The special recipe contained something secret to make them stay crunchy for months in damp conditions. It was probably best if no one enquired about the unknown ingredient, especially as it appeared to be addictive.

It didn't matter what time of day or night, if those biscuits were not sitting in any of his dishes he would behave in such a way that his demands were met. But he didn't yowl or cry for his biscuits. He indicated that he expected to be fed by noisily tapping his paw on the lid of the container and then stalked about staring menacingly with a mean, scary look. Anyone in the houses knew what they had to do, or else. His dish had to be fully replenished with fresh biscuits right up to the rim, *every* time. A half ration was no good to him. No point just giving the stale ones a noisy jiggle in the almost empty dish or rattling the tin from a distance while calling out "Biiiiiiiss-kiiiiiiitts!" then adding a measly few fresh ones as a top layer.

It was impossible to trick Cat Biskit Davy with these sound effects or lazy attempts at economising.

He was the wisest cat ever. He knew his own mind. He could not be persuaded to do something he didn't want to or be somewhere he didn't want to. If anyone told him to move off their chair or bed he remained completely still and glowered at them with his 'Cat Biskit' stare. It was *they* who had to find another place to sit, lie down and relax or, most likely, sulk. He lived quietly and determinedly as if every day's agenda was planned, merely moving slowly and mysteriously between his various homes. But no one ever saw him after midnight or before dawn.

Not one human being knew quite what Cat Biskit Davy would actually do if his biscuits weren't properly topped up; an unnerving look about him hinted he may have magical powers and no one wanted to risk those. Narrowing his eyes in a frown-like stare at those humans was as though he were reading their thoughts – that is when he paid any attention at all to fellow housemates. His disapproving glances as he wandered about may not have meant to have left his keepers feeling they were unimportant or didn't exist, but this was the effect Davy had on everyone – that the inferior human species was far beneath his own intelligence and importance.

Furthermore, as well as being treated with disapproval, humans were uneasy about his secret nocturnal life. His regular habit was to return home very tired just before the sun came up as though he was avoiding bright daylight.

He didn't sunbathe on the window sill either, something most cats enjoy. Instead, he slept in a sunless room near an open fire as soon as he had filled his tum. He remained there snoring until noon when it was time for more cat biscuits. Each new owner (or more accurately, 'feeder') accepted that he was not affectionate and that their relationship was more that the householder were 'employed' by the cat as a servant. In truth, he must have felt sad and lonely, suddenly finding himself in a strange unfamiliar place where he knew no one and missed everything about his former life. He popped up all over the place, yet no one had any idea where he'd appeared from. The local population had no clue he was from a wrecked Caribbean ship.

At the clifftop cottage Arabella had found and rented for her recently widowed uncle, Cat Biskit Davy eventually walked in one night from the blustery darkness during a wild lightning storm. He found the quiet, gentle nature of his new companion suited his requirements, not knowing that he was in any way connected to his mistress, Arabella. He didn't even know for sure if she had survived, if she was in hiding or had by now hopped on board another vessel and was back at sea. The deafening roar of the churning sea lashing on the rocks nearby was no wonder anything which lived outside would have wished to be inside that night. Even White Owl, usually happy in the snug hollow of his nearby oak tree, found a gap under the eaves of the house and, for once, slept snuggly in the new occupant's attic.

A week or so before that stormy night a wooden ship had been wrecked on those rocks and was found next morning. A piece of the ship lay on its side on the beach. The bunks where the crew had slept were miraculously unharmed, lying wedged in a broken section of the ship in the sand. But no sign of life, not even bodies or shoes. The ship's maps from Arabella's cabin, which had made a snug cat bed, were now scattered the length of the beach. The villagers said the ship's flag was floating on its broken pole. Painted on the flag was a palm tree, the initials 'AD' and a funny drawing of a black eye mask.

Although the locals would not normally be familiar with foreign ships' flags, the one they found was the symbol of the feared and dangerous female pirate Arabella Davy, known to have settled in the Caribbean islands. No doubting it was her ship, commandeered from some unfortunate crew. Her distinctive flag had been spotted on the 'Reward' notices posted outside the taverns. She had sailed all over the world stealing treasure from ships and killing any of the mariners who tried to stop her. The villagers, of course, had no idea what she looked like as an adult because she'd involuntarily left Cornwall as an infant with her young mother after a kidnapping raid. And thereby hangs another story.

Arabella was the legendary sister of local fisherman, Tristan Davy, who years earlier had been wrongly but deliberately arrested and dealt with harshly by the authorities; she had returned to England wanting justice for her brother. He lived simply and had nothing to do with the smuggling or the clandestine goings-on. He was a loner and had always kept his nose clean. The locals wondered if this infamous female pirate could now be in their midst, having survived this latest shipwreck caused by the fierce gale.

Cats quite often appear in new households during or after a storm. On this occasion, my ancestor who was renting the old house above the beach, had just moved in, and knew he had been adopted out of the blue with no choice in the matter. That's how cats are. People say it is the cat who chooses the person and where they live. If they stick close to one person and show affection it's because they have chosen them. A great honour. A silent declaration of trust.

A cat 'keeper' might provide every requirement for survival, but one cannot 'own' a cat. The cat can leave for good at any moment and sometimes do, having selected another home, having given it a quick once-over or a long trial run. They might pop back with a few friends to lie out in the sun, have a wash and a snack and then go back to their new place. Preferring different biscuits or just the sound of the new name they are called could be all it takes for defecting – a perfect double life consisting of two evening meals, two distinct atmospheres, two comfy beds… and two names just like a secret agent. No chance of getting bored if each keeper is competing, doing everything in their power to pamper the defector, hoping to win them back permanently.

Needless to say, Cat Biskit Davy was huge but not necessarily fat; he was just a very big cat and his black fur was lush. A big, black, fluffy cat, although he was disproving of the word 'fluffy' to describe him. Immediately he heard the word his eyes, pale yellow as the moon and as big as saucers, scarily narrowed to slits. He had a very serious face, much more humanlike than feline. Some cats appear as if they are smiling sweetly but no one ever saw

Cat Biskit Davy smile. He seemed to have a reputation to maintain.

Davy walked about proudly wearing a diamond collar with a silver medallion. On one side the name 'DAVY' had been engraved. On the other, symbols of the moon and stars with a skull and crossbones were visible. No one knew who engraved this medallion as one couldn't get close enough to actually read the name without a menacing *hiss!* It was pretty obvious Cat Biskit Davy had a secret, if not several, which he hoped to keep to himself at the mysterious meeting in the woods he'd been invited to while out for a stroll through the moonlit trees.

The Secret Society of Cats had each made their way across the higgledy-piggledy clifftop pathways waiting for their newest member to arrive. They met in the smuggling tunnels beneath two homes named The Crow's Nest which was Dr Watts' house and Pixie Cottage, the one which Arabella had just acquired for her uncle. The group had expected to get on with a quiet meeting involving no smuggling activities. They huddled together high up in their little bunker where the long white candles were stored to light the passageways. This metal cupboard had a door with holes drilled at the top allowing them to sit on the top shelf, side by side in a

row. From here they could spy on the smugglers' shenanigans through the air holes without being seen. The Secret Society of Cats had very sad and special reasons for teaming up and for watching these scallywags at work.

Everything had to be done by the smuggling thieves at lightning speed and in total silence to avoid getting caught by the law or reported by anyone spying on them looking for a reward. Rowing out towards the ship in the blackness for the floating barrels, rolling them up the beach into the cave and hurtling them through the tunnel carrying such weight was a fast and slick operation. They wore identical coloured jerkins and breeches so, if observed, they could not be identified at the scene of the crime by their clothing. They also wore very soft soled suede boots to avoid making any sound. The directions for manoeuvring the treasure would only be given by hand signals. When they'd finished storing the loot in Dr Watts' cellar, each smuggler scattered in a different direction through the dense thickets on the clifftop so that none were discovered heading home together.

The Spaniards Inn was the only place they could enjoy a tankard of beer to plan the next escapade without neighbours getting suspicious. The isolated location of the inn was high on a solitary, windy ridge, well away from the village. The intense roar of the sea up there was not a welcoming atmosphere. Before meeting again, after hiding away their stolen goods, the smugglers would wait another day until the coast was clear and the ship involved had safely set sail, out of sight. Sometimes the ship's captain would know about the barrels being stolen and often it was done after he had gone to sleep. On the one hand, whichever way the plot had been arranged, with his knowledge or without it, he would need to turn a blind eye if he wished to stay safe among his men. On the other hand, if the authorities found out about the source of the stolen goods, the consequences could end his entire well-paid career and his reputation, resulting in financial ruin and death in poverty.

Chapter Three

The Secret Society of Cats

"Where on earth is he?" *Merlin* asked impatiently.

"Before I arrived in here, I saw him stalking past the entrance and I presumed he was going in," *Magic* remembered, not really concentrating, half watching the huge drops dripping from the ceiling to make sure none landed on him. Those drops didn't look like water. No one took much notice as he often claimed to have seen things that no one else had. The others were never sure if he was talking mumbo jumbo or whether he had mystical visions, and he actually didn't really care what they thought.

"We cannot begin without our guest because he is the reason we are having this extra 'extraordinary' meeting. We have to make sure he is one of us."

K-L-A-A-A-N-G-G-G!

They almost jumped out of their skins. A loud clatter from the beach end of the dark tunnel startled them because they were not expecting anything to happen that night. Normally it was totally silent inside, even if the north wind was blowing; this was because the doors at either end were heavy and the tunnel was dug out of thick slate, the kind of shiny grey stone found on a roof. The smugglers obviously didn't realise there was yet another smaller undisclosed passage The Secret Society of Cats had found.

The cats squeezed in from the coal cellar in the garden of *Cat Biskit Davy*'s new house. It was the perfect hideaway for them whenever the weather was bad. It had a plentiful supply of mice who, unfortunately for them, had the same idea of coming in out of the rain.

The smugglers were only aware of the tunnel which began in a small watery cave; this was where a couple of boats were hidden to row out to the wrecked ships. The tunnel led directly from the beach right up into Dr Watts' house. The spooky three-storey house was named The Crow's Nest after the small lookout platform at the top of a ship's mast where a sailor with a telescope kept watch to sight land or attackers out at sea. Dr Watts kept watch in exactly the

same way from his attic window in the tower whenever one of their smuggling sprees was about to happen. He could see for miles up there, as far as the horizon. He had a bird's-eye view of any friend or enemy heading his way in a ship. And to think the entire village thought that Dr 'la-di-da' Watts was so trusted and respectable.

Crow was his tame crow who flew out to the ships like a carrier pigeon. He would carry a message in secret code fixed to his leg giving the expected location and time of the ship's docking. The doctor guided the ship into the safe side of the bay below his house by waving a lantern from side to side from his turret.

Merlin ordered everyone into their safe cupboard and sent *Moonie* down to investigate the startling noise they'd heard at the far end of the passage. He soon trotted back up the steep slope saying that there was no sign of their new guest but that one of the metal candle holders on the wall had mysteriously fallen off.

Celestine asked if *Cat Biskit Davy* knew how to find them.

"Maybe he's inside and got lost. There's no light in here. This secret passage between the gardens of these two houses is even harder to find if you've never been in here before."

Moonie then got sent up to the top of the small passage and, sure enough, there was *Davy* outside, pacing up and down in the cellar wondering how to get in. He had the jitters, having seen something which really worried him. *Crow* had just flown overhead, flying westward, not his normal route over the moor. Travelling westward only went out to the vast sea which was so huge – no land in sight until France. Was he lost? Would he have enough puff to return home with nowhere to take refuge to rest?

Moonie explained about their top secret air vent access over the entrance door. Davy would have to squash himself very small to get through it, which worried him because he was bigger than the others. He would feel very stupid if he got stuck. The passage door itself was made to look like a stone wall. From the outside it cleverly blended into the cellar wall as though part of it, with no visible gaps where the door ended or the wall began. That hidden passage had existed for quite some years but had been boarded up for safety by previous owners who were not smugglers. This was unusual for ordinary folk in such a small village because, with little honest work available and high taxes making each necessity hard to afford, everyone tended to be involved. It became normality, even with serious risks if caught. Most people at least bought food or brandy, pretending they didn't know if it was stolen.

In one way or another, everyone in the area had to be in on the secret because smugglers on beaches never knew who might be peeping from behind rocks to see them in action or observe them on their way home in the dead of night. Sometimes the very people responsible for catching and handing out punishment were part of the gang too, like sheriffs and tax inspectors. They would help distribute and sell irresistible luxuries to their friends, making heaps of money on top of their pay. These exchanges were made for cash, gold coins or perhaps swapping one luxury for another.

Moonie and *Davy* arrived from the top of the passage and *Merlin* asked the others to introduce themselves.

"Hello," welcomed *Celestine* in her exotic accent. "I'm a blue Persian, as you can see, and I live in Moonlit Cove with Miss Mannequin, the dressmaker."

"I am *Magic*, said the blonde Romany cat. "I adopted the lady who owns The Curiosity Shop because I love being surrounded by sparkling jewels."

The other black cat who had fetched *Davy* spoke next:

"*Moonie* is my Society name, but my real name is Timmins, which *Merlin* thought not bold enough for someone so expert at catching mice for our banquets. I live with the butcher.

Cat Biskit Davy shuddered; he felt sick at the thought.

"I am called *Starlight*," purred the only other female. She was a silver-grey tabby distinctively marked with a bold white star on her chest.

So there they were – five were soon to be six. The Half Moon Bay Secret Society of Cats: *Merlin, Magic, Moonie, Celestine* and *Starlight.*

Cat Biskit Davy wondered what would happen next, what they expected of him. He wasn't sure if he was going to like this way of life, he wasn't used to being in one place on land or mixing with other cats! He had been born on a ship, used to the sea almost all of his life – that's when he wasn't on a warm tropical island surrounded by palms and coconut trees. He doubted if they realised how he had come to be there and wondered if it might be unwise to reveal his misadventure.

"Well," *Merlin* began his announcement, "to be in our Society, first of all you must catch three mice."

"Shiver me timbers," muttered *Davy* in his soft lilting accent.

"I beg your pardon; is there something wrong with catching mice?" *Merlin* asked, looking quite put out.

"Well, yes! There is, because I'm a vegetarian. My name is Cat *BISKIT* Davy," he said proudly, emphasising 'biscuit' – "and not for no reason."

"Oooooh," squealed *Celestine*, "I know all about them, Miss Mannequin is one of those."

"Mmmmm," grumbled *Merlin*, "well, this is going to be very difficult. The whole idea is this: you have to prove yourself to be silent and quick to be part of our club – a hunter. Part of our job is helping keep watch while the smuggling is going on so we can help ourselves to anything interesting. Sometimes whole barrels of fish come up these passages and get left unattended, enough time to pinch a few."

"Stone the crows!" His fur visibly shuddered again.

"I can assure you, sir, that the only thing I hunt is biscuits," protested *Davy*.

Elderly *Merlin* wiggled his white whiskers. His eyes narrowed and flickered, staring suspiciously at his young junior.

"Don't tell me there's something wrong with fish, too?"

How was *Cat Biskit Davy* going to reveal the truth to his new contacts? A ship's cat who hates mice and fish. And there was more.

"Yes. I am sorry to say I have never eaten a fish and I will not be able to join your Society because I have my own secret which is sure to be even worse than *not* eating meat or fish." It all came out in a rush for he was keen for his comrades to know about him now. "I am a shipwrecked cat. I was washed up on the beach in part of a ship and I belong to a famous pirate who will one day be back for me, I know it. I belong to Arabella Davy, Pirate Queen of the Seven Seas. When we are not at sea we live on a very warm, sunny island of palm trees surrounded by soft white sand and shimmering turquoise water."

There was a stony silence while each cat looked slowly at the other and then all eyes were on *Cat Biskit Davy*.

"Yes, everyone has heard of Arabella, she was originally born here and, yes, we *know*," whispered *Celestine* kindly, "and we guessed you couldn't understand why we invited you. We are *all* shipwrecked cats and all once belonged to pirates, whom we hope may come back for us, too. We are not sure if they drowned or escaped and are temporarily land-locked, waiting to join a safe ship to return to sea. This is why we sit watching the smugglers running up and down the tunnels, hoping to see our owners or the crew who work for them. Then we could make a dash for the rowing boats and return to our companions."

Davy was astonished. He was not as unique as he had believed. So this abandonment was one of the sad consequences of shipwrecks, especially deliberate ones.

All of a sudden there was another clatter from the far end of the tunnel followed by a gush of wind. They hunched their shoulders and half closed their eyes against the cold blast which curled their whiskers.

Merlin quickly beckoned them all back into the bunker and pulled the door shut with his paw.

"Don't anyone breathe. We weren't expecting anyone in here tonight."

Unexpectedly, a slim figure wearing a huge feathered hat pulled down over his face carrying a lighted torch, ran past their cupboard and down the tunnel leading to the beach. Luckily, he didn't need any more of the candles kept in their hideout. The shadowy figure had come in through the cellar door at the top of the passage and was opening the creaking wooden beach door by turning the concealed handle in the wall. Was he letting others in from the beach?

'So that was why it had fallen,' *Merlin* thought to himself. 'That terrible crash that had us jumping out of our skins – someone had found the handle to the secret door earlier.'

The feline group could see several figures coming through the archway from the beach but no one was carrying anything.

One of them came so close to where they were hiding it appeared as though they were about to open their cupboard. Instead, the figure in the hat stood completely pressed against their door, reaching above it, straining to remove the loose bricks in the wall. None of the cats dared breathe for quite some moments. *Celestine* just about managed to stop herself sneezing. One by one, the rest of the men who had entered from the beach lifted down the hidden barrels and went up and out of the top exit through the cellar door.

'Oh,' thought *Magic,* remembering not to speak out loud, 'that's what those drips were all about – there's some real jiggery-pokery going on here.'

It was clear there was no incoming cargo tonight; instead someone else had discovered the hiding place of the last shipment and had come to steal everything before it got moved on and sold.

The Secret Society of Cats lay very still and quiet, some gulping with fear, all except *Davy* who could smell something familiar. He could not quite believe his little wet nose… the warm, mysterious perfume worn by Arabella Davy. The man in the feathered hat… could it possibly have been..? He was afraid the others would hear his heart pounding with excitement.

But all hell had broken out at the top exit – raised angry voices and agitated horses' hooves stamping on the cobbles outside. The Secret Society would now have to remain motionless for some considerable time to come.

Chapter Four

Arabella's Dangerous Return to England

Arabella may have been brave and fearless but she was still wanted in many countries, including England, for piracy. Returning to rescue her brother from prison meant she was risking her neck should she be caught while remaining there due to her capsized ship.

The local king's magistrate, Judge Julian, who had tried and punished her brother years earlier, was involved in the smuggling gang. Stolen goods were stored in his home and he had sent Tristan Davy to prison to get him out of the way, only because he was suspected of having overheard their plans at the inn, which he had most certainly not. Tristan had no idea that the police, the magistrate, sheriff and local doctor had all been involved for years. His punishment was extra harsh because he'd been sent away across the world to Australia where the magistrate hoped no one would ever hear from him again. Quite possibly his biggest mistake was that he was *not* involved in the smuggling network of his fishing village which made him suspicious to those that were.

Pirates have their contacts and friends everywhere – they sail the seven seas of the globe after all. There is no corner of the world a pirate cannot find or find out about. Word soon spread as to where Tristan was and why. Soon his daring, protective sibling would also hear the whole story. She was an amazingly loyal sister to have. She was slim and beautiful and had no fear of anyone at all. She did not fear the wild storms at sea, miles from any land. She did not fear the most dangerous male pirates. And she had made friends with many of them because she had grown up in their world and they respected her bravery. They were in fierce competition with one another. It was the fastest race to any ship carrying something worth stealing. She even considered taking captive the fit and healthy crew to sell as servants in another country.

Centuries ago, pirates were known to sneak up at night in their ships and take away everyone from tiny fishing villages along the coasts of Ireland, England and even Iceland, carrying them to faraway lands where their life would be very different. And herewith hangs a tale of how Arabella and her young widowed mother found themselves across the Atlantic Ocean in the Caribbean islands, thousands of miles from home.

Arabella was determined to rescue her brother but first had to seek out the policeman who arrested him. She knew he held information essential to achieve her aim. Since her ship was wrecked on the beach at Half Moon Bay, she went into hiding on the moors where she met the mysterious owner of the Spaniards Inn trudging home. Curiously, he did not hesitate in taking her home to his wife to get her dry and cleaned up, changing from her pirate clothing into more suitable attire that would go unnoticed in an English village.

It was this couple who told Arabella about the ideal empty cottage overlooking the beach. No one would suspect her identity once dressed as an Englishwoman, and the innkeepers just happened to own the empty house for rent. At first she could only pay them offerings of the jewels she kept strapped in a leather pouch hidden in her undergarments. But once she had sold some of the treasures to a regular traveller who stopped at the inn she had plenty of cash to last for her temporary stay in Cornwall. Meanwhile she attended to the matter regarding her brother; raising funds to sail to his rescue was another hurdle yet to face.

Before taking up residence at her new temporary address, she had made her way to the heart of the village to find her widowed uncle living in a tiny rented room since his wife had died. Arabella moved him into the spacious old stone cottage and spent a few days making it homely. She was good at adapting to new living conditions and making the best of them. Improving the dullest of homes or a ship's cabin to look cosy and inviting was a particular gift of hers despite her fierce nature. During her short stay, Bella sat outside for hours at a time painting the sea views from the cottage garden but not because she was a good artist. The garden overlooked the beach from where she could overhear many discussions below her, plotting when ship raids would take place. Arabella also heard the names of many important local characters, too. These were music to her ears and especially considering she learnt exactly who was behind the highly organised conspiracy regarding her brother. She needed to know where that person might be found.

Bold as ever, Arabella only slightly changed her name and when she renamed Pixie Cottage she proudly hung up the sign: BELLA VISTA, meaning 'pretty view'. The words could also have meant 'Bella's view'. Pirates can be like that; they love to take risks while laughing at those they are out to get or those out to get them, living right under the noses of the authorities who wish to arrest or get even with them while they are disguised as someone else. And not too disguised in her case.

Arabella was about to set off on a long overland journey. She had people to find and informed her uncle she would be back when she had finished all she needed to do. Perhaps weeks, perhaps a month or so. He was disappointed to be left alone again no matter how spacious the house, how beautiful the garden and the view out to sea. He had been waiting a long time to be reunited with her and now she was going again. Her uncle had little idea of her escapades or that, during her pirate raids, Arabella often disguised herself as a man. Her long, curly hair was tightly tucked up in a scarf under her distinctive hat with its floating white ostrich plume. It was legendary in the pirate world how shocked her victims were when she jumped on board a ship they had taken in an attack

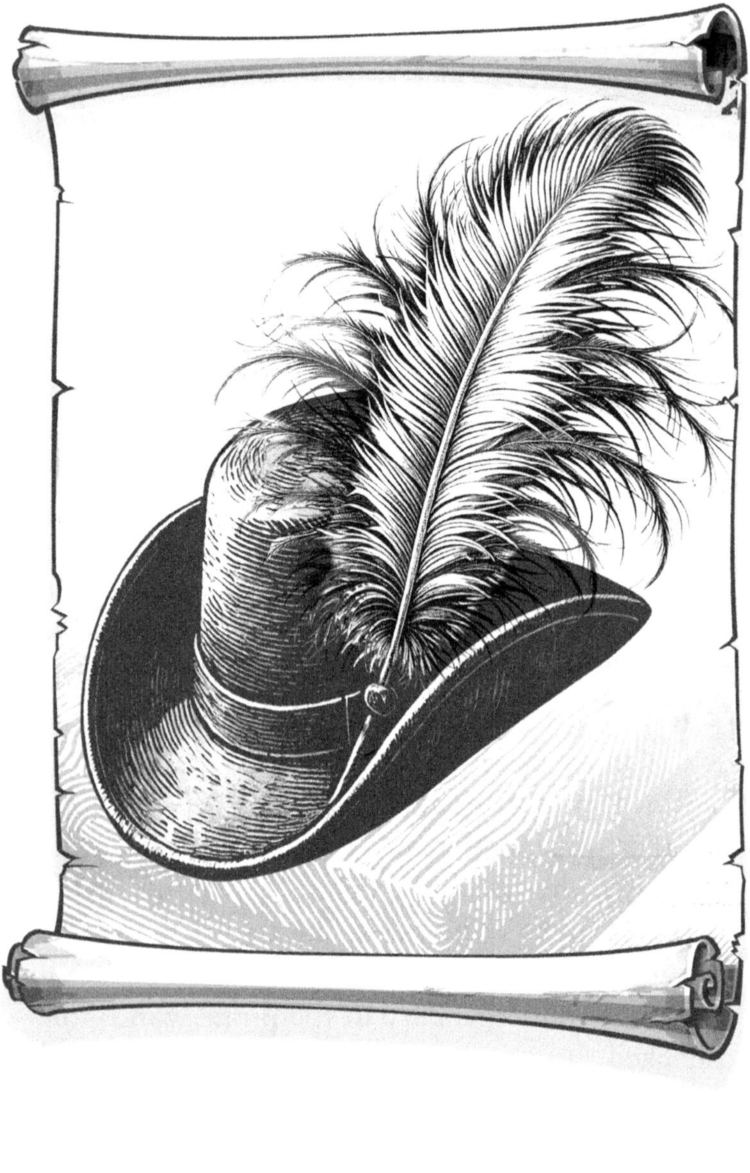

and, without hesitation, drew her sword. Over the side they went – Arabella's eyes gleaming with satisfaction.

If she managed to kill an evil captain she stood with one foot on his chest, waving her feathered hat triumphantly in the air and letting her long hair tumble down, just to shock the rest he'd been killed by a woman. This effect had guaranteed her victory because no man wanted to risk their reputation in life or death. They often threw down their weapons and gave themselves up. They wanted to carry on pirating. The treasure was hers. They would rather be taken captive and work for her than leave a legacy that they'd been killed by her.

The more romantic amongst them passed on tales that she always left a strong, lingering, hypnotic aroma wherever she had been. Her perfume came from an exotic land full of jewels and beautiful things which people all over the world wanted to own. Arabella was victorious over and over again because she had patiently planned her raids with great detail. Everyone on board knew in advance exactly the part they had to play and she always recruited the best crew for their unique and cunning skills. Quite a number of her crew were women who fought as bloodily as the men.

Arabella planned everything meticulously, writing down what she needed to achieve with numbered, step by step actions and instructions to help her prepare mentally and single-mindedly. This strategy never failed her – whether it was overcoming a problem, creating a beautiful garment or fighting a battle. Above all, she remembered her grandmother's wisdom to never be impulsive, that patience is a virtue – never rush decisions to regret them later. In addition, she knew she had to decide on the next move cautiously and always have a good night's sleep to be able to think clearly before giving a response or writing to anyone about any important matter. Her grandmother had also advised that her intuition, her 'gut' feeling, would also serve her well when making decisions in life.

By listening to her heart to how her senses reacted to certain people, to unexpected news or a sudden change in circumstances, would often swiftly get her out of trouble. Her grandmother's wisest words of all were that if Bella had to question herself more than once whether a certain person was truly a loyal friend, then they most likely were not.

Finally, she kept a diary. Late at night in the sanctuary of her creaking cabin, writing and planning was the perfect way to while away the long sea journeys that went on for weeks. The soothing, warm glow of candlelight made the ritual of writing down her thoughts about friends, foes, worries and successes more powerful. Whenever she was uncertain of a character she would re-read the words written in her diary weeks or months before... and jumping from the page was a warning message, a repeated pattern of curious behaviour. Her earlier fears about a suspicious person's false intentions had now come true and it was time to act instead of pretending to herself all was well. Arabella must either have no further contact or play along with them as though she trusted them. They would eventually reveal their own skulduggery and cause their own downfall rather than hers. And just to confirm her suspicions were correct, her beloved cat would stretch sleepily beside her, letting out a grunt as though reading her mind, which he probably was.

Cat Biskit Davy had been part of her devoted crew; he certainly was a very loyal cabin companion to her and she had missed him greatly. In the same way she promised to find her brother and set him free, she was also searching for her beloved feline friend. He was as important to her as anything in her life because he depended on her for his survival and happiness. She simply would not accept abandoning him without a very long and thorough search. Arabella was unaware he had been thinking of retiring from pirating and was seeking a quieter life. She had no idea if he had by now already used up all of his nine lives during the dangerous battles they had been involved in. She hoped with all her heart that he, like her, had survived their shipwreck and had taken refuge somewhere. Without mentioning she was searching for her own cat, she promised anyone nearby whom she trusted that on ever discovering a black cat, feeding him or her would bring them tremendous good fortune. And being a Cornish village where superstitions were part of life, this well-planned rumour spread fast.

Chapter Five

Unexpected Betrayal

Back inside the tunnel, barrels of expensive French brandy were being rolled up the passage and not down to the beach as The Secret Society of Cats would expect to see. They wondered how on earth these raiders were avoiding being seen by the new occupants of 'Bella Vista' cottage.

Celestine almost sneezed again. Something pungent in the air was causing her allergy. Outside they could hear the *clippity-clop* of horses' hooves and the heavy wooden wheels from a carriage trundling over the cobblestones at the entrance to the cottage. So *this* is where these barrels were going. They were not going out to sea as they had previously heard discussed.

Moonie took a sharp intake of breath as another figure loomed closer to their cupboard door to take down the last barrel of brandy from above them. He recognised the man as the owner of the Spaniards Inn. *Moonie* had sheltered up there for a while after he got lost on the moors following his terrible experience when his wrecked ship washed up overnight. He had been asleep in a hammock and when he woke he was still in the hammock, except it was full of sea water on a blustery English beach.

Moonie had wearily made his way over the scary, deserted, prickly heathland on the moor by heading in the direction of the yellow glow of lights from the inn. Mysteriously, someone there had put out food for him each night as though they were expecting him and, eventually, they allowed him inside.

He heard people discussing the innkeeper's mystifying past. How he just appeared. He turned up and took over the premises after the previous owner had left just as suddenly, not mentioning to anyone he intended to leave. No one ever knew what had happened to him. And now *Moonie* was beginning to think something bad. Maybe he had been a pirate, too. The new landlord gave no clues as to where he was from himself or how he came by the tenancy. Might he have killed the previous innkeeper? Such was the sinister mystery of the place that the regular drinkers dared not ask. True locals did not tend to frequent the place for long. Thirsty casual labourers from the fields would nip in and knock back one quick drink, but dash straight back to their lodgings without conversation or eye contact with anyone else. But on the night of The Secret Society's extra 'extraordinary' meeting, here was the new innkeeper off duty and just inches away from them in the gloomy, airless tunnel, already mixed up in a very dangerous situation.

Moonie knew that the rest of the smugglers met up in the inn's back room to plan their raids and that one of those regular drinkers was the horrible magistrate, Judge Julian, who felt safe there because no one respectable from the village went in. It was mainly used as a stage, a stop for coach passengers passing through in the carriages pulled by horses on their way to or from London. Observant *Moonie* discovered that a barrel or two of something stolen often found its way onto those carriages to London. And now he was discovering where the supply was probably from. Thieves robbing other thieves, perhaps?

"Oright, me old mate – get this load up to the inn. There's a carriage leaving for London in the morning," ordered the character *Moonie* recognised as the new innkeeper. Same distinctive London accent.

"You see?" he told the other felines, "the new owner of the Spaniards Inn has stolen the stuff stored down here by the doctor and is sending it to London. I wonder who tipped him off where it was kept?"

Outside the cellar, *Magic* stood guard on the stone wall of the doctor's house and let out a piercing *meeow!* just as *Bounty,* the Sheriff's mare, approached along the lane, making her rear up onto her hind legs and stop. She knew something was wrong and that *Magic* needed help.

Magic thumped down onto the ground on all fours just in front of *Bounty*, ran a few steps and then stopped and howled again, which certainly got Sheriff Parson's attention. He ran a few steps and stopped again repeatedly until the Sheriff dismounted to follow him. First, he gently led *Bounty* to the gate to tie her there. *Magic* walked quickly with his tail up, leaving the curious officer under no doubt he was being led to something important. In the courtyard of the cottage, they found the usually locked hidden door slightly open, with loud voices coming from inside. The officer could not believe his luck. The familiar voices were shouting accusations at one another. In their anger these men had totally forgotten to be careful of being seen and heard.

The Sheriff drew his pistol while silently creeping inside the entrance of the tunnel. To his amazement, he found the normally calm gentleman doctor and the local magistrate almost fighting with each other, their faces red with anger.

"You have cheated me, you scoundrel!" shouted the magistrate, Judge Julian.

"Ha! So now you know how it feels!" the doctor yelled back. "You've never heard of honour among thieves? I suspected you were regularly taking a barrel for yourself without telling me, but how did you think you would get away with…"

He trailed off at the sound of the Sheriff cocking his pistol as if about to fire at them, at the same time eyeing the gaping hole in the wall above their heads where the brandy had once been hidden. The suspects were ordered to put their hands above their heads and not move.

Both the doctor and the magistrate had been watching the cottage from separate locations and had seen Arabella and her uncle leave at different times earlier that evening. The doctor intended to take the brandy he was meant to share with the magistrate and the rest of the smugglers, but it was already gone. Even more curious was that the magistrate had exactly the same idea to take all of it for himself to sell. And funnier still, yet another person had got there before either of them.

A loud knock on the door at the bottom of the tunnel startled everyone. A male dressed exactly like one of the most wanted, notorious pirates crept in but was shocked to see the sight of the distinctive Sheriff armed with a pistol. He ran for his life back down the tunnel and out along the beach empty-handed. Without stopping, he ran right around the bay and into Moonlit Cove to where his ship had been waiting for the consignment.

It appeared the doctor had cheated everyone. *Crow* had earlier taken a message from the doctor to the ship anchored out of sight in Moonlit Cove, telling the crew the tunnel would be open for them to take the brandy barrels for which they would pay only him, but the doctor arrived to take the payment to find the stash already gone. The two furious men continued to yell accusations at one another.

"Quiet!' shouted the Sheriff. "Hands above your heads!" he yelled as he deliberately set aim at them.

The pair raised their hands without hesitation, their mouths falling open, eyes out on stalks, fully expecting to be shot. Throughout the drama, The Secret Society of Cats were trembling inside their cupboard, all wishing they had been the one to wait outside to alert Sheriff Parsons, as *Magic* had done, and so admirably. Still at his post, his feline senses could feel the vibration through the ground of the horses' hooves galloping in their direction long before they came into sight. The Sheriff's men were on their way.

Still pointing his pistol at the two culprits, but aware any gunshots inside the tunnel would bury them all alive, he demanded an explanation.

"Aah! Dr Watts, I presume. And it's you! Judge Julian, no less. I really have caught two important birds with one stone. Can you explain what you are both doing down here in your new neighbour's home, Doctor? And in particular, in their well hidden cellar? Those look like splashes of brandy on the floor… certainly smells like it. *And* there's something else lingering in the air – smells like spice, or is it vanilla? …or both …mmm. What else have you two been smuggling?" He seemed to close his eyes and drift off for a moment, still with gun in hand.

He breathed in deeply as though in a trance, seemingly concentrating on identifying the delicious aroma. The pistol drooped in his hand

and swung loosely from his thumb. The cats gazed in disbelief. For a scary moment it looked as if the villains might escape. *Merlin* noisily rattled the candles in the tin box, bringing the hero of the moment back to his senses. He waved the captives outside, shocked at how easily they gave in – not the bravest of men he had encountered, but luckily for his own safety, neither possessed a gun.

The rest of his mounted officers clattered into the usually tranquil cobbled courtyard and tied each of the villains onto a horse with their hands behind their backs. They were on their way to jail. The pair would have so many questions to answer. No doubt plenty of villagers and other dignitaries would be willing to speak against them now the high-ups were in disgrace and their wrongly jailed relatives would even be freed.

As the *clippity-clop!* of hooves faded into the distance, The Secret Society of Cats were safe to come out of their uncomfortable hiding place. They had been in the dark for much longer than usual due to the kerfuffle with this double-crossing gang.

They could all feel the draught from the door to the beach through which that lone pirate had scarpered. They discussed their options for the safest escape route, presuming a police constable was possibly on guard duty. Scurrying along the beach in the darkness was not a good idea, so they sneaked up to the cellar door expecting to see a constable or two. Sure enough, there were two officers but they were chatting and smoking across the road. The courtyard was clear; its wall gave them adequate cover as they slinked out onto the clifftop path.

Moonie warned the others that under the cottage was definitely not a safe place to meet for sometime.

"With what is going on, the entire village of smugglers might turn up one by one, looking for their share of the brandy, and all we've got left is that stinking barrel of rotting fish over there. Would you like one, *Starlight*?"

"That's not funny," she protested. "You have a very strange sense of humour, if I may say. I shall make my way to Miss Mannequin for a lovely French meal. She mentioned someone else coming for dinner."

"'We've got Les Cargo tonight', I think she said."

"Well, make sure to stick to Bluebell Path over the cliff; don't cut across the beach while there's a ship still anchored out there even though that way may be quicker as the crow flies," warned her friend.

The humans used this crow expression to mean taking a very direct route with no bends or hills or going 'all round the houses', which is another old expression for taking ages to get somewhere.

Cat Biskit Davy believed he had smelt Arabella's fragrance in the tunnel. She was very superstitious that the potion kept her safe and brought her luck. He had not been certain if it was purposely hypnotic, that is, until tonight.

Moonie meandered back to the butcher's house where his meal would be waiting in his dish. He was sure that all those barrels had already made their way up to the Spaniards Inn and that the Sheriff may be paying the inn a visit. It looked pretty obvious that the new innkeeper himself had spied on the secret smuggler meetings in the back room, but there was no way of knowing whom was on whose side. Nevertheless, tonight had been a revelation that there was no one left to be trusted. The Society had arranged to meet together the following night in a safe place in the woods to discuss whatever they had found out from listening to the humans' conversations in the cats' respective homes overnight. News of the arrests would be all over the village in less than an hour. *Davy* felt he would be safe upstairs with

Spaniards
INN

the elderly man who had only recently moved in, but he had no idea there was also a female tenant because she had gone again before he'd found the house. The Sheriff had left the new tenant a note that he would call on him in the morning to explain the serious incident and arrest. It had taken place on his premises and he intended to take a statement from him.

With an auspicious full moon high in the sky, The Secret Society of Cats set off for their homes in the bright silver light feeling very exhausted. Each hoped there'd be a future vote to find a new meeting place. They still had to keep an eye on the smuggling pirates to try to get back to their own seafaring human companions. Due to their special ceremony to accept and welcome a new member becoming disrupted, and with *Cat Biskit Davy*'s similar tale to their own, he had won a place in their kind hearts and was now one of them – all without having to catch a mouse or eat a fish!

Cat Biskit Davy didn't mention to the others that he had sensed the presence of Arabella as the barrels were being lifted from the wall above them. While the others dashed away, relieved to be getting home, he hung back.

Chapter Six

Cat Biskit Davy Completely Disappears

The tunnels were as black as coal when the candles had gone out but *Davy* felt he was so close to finding Arabella that he overcame his fear of the dark and the unknown.

He followed the current of cold sea air that masked any other scent to wherever she had been. The passage went on and on and he suddenly realised the smell of the sea and the stiff breeze were not as strong. In the pitch-black he had unwittingly taken a fork into another narrower, twisting tunnel. He had no idea where he was. He stiffened with fear and his hackles stood on end. Why on earth had he made this decision? It must have been obvious she had gone to supervise wherever the barrels had been taken.

But wherever she was, he could now smell

her scent in this stuffy, claustrophobic tunnel and, as the Sheriff had mentioned, a strange waft of spice, too. Perhaps this was where she was hiding before the raid took place. Maybe she would return here. He did his best to retrace his steps back up to the cellar but kept finding himself in another tunnel as though going round in circles. This was a clever way for smugglers to hide their loot. Anyone unfamiliar with the layout would not find their way to it and certainly not the way out. The smugglers would leave secret chalk marks on the walls to help them find their way.

Davy's nose twitched. At last he was getting another telltale aroma that he was nearing the cellar exit. He could smell the horses…

He worried about his size by squeezing through the air vent without anyone there to assist in case he got stuck. As he eased his way through, he caught his diamond collar on the grille. He could neither go forward nor back and he let out a yelp. This alerted the constables outside who came to investigate. Now he was done for!

Next night the rest of the Society meet in the woods inside White Owl's hollow oak, but *Davy* doesn't appear.

Magic decides immediately he must go in search of *Davy* even though they all believe returning to the cellar could be extremely dangerous. The types of people who may be on guard were not renowned for their kindness to animals.

"The Sheriff will have made it out of bounds and it might be boarded up," exclaimed *Moonie*.

"Or get boarded up with nails and planks while any of us are inside," added *Starlight*, always the optimist.

"Well, all the more reason to find out where he is and if he's safe. Why on earth have we formed a Secret Society if we don't watch out for each other?" *Magic* retorted impatiently. Just as he had not hesitated in bravely halting *Bounty* to bring the attention of the Sheriff to the skulduggery in the cellar, he took leave of his companions. It was up to them to decide to go with him or not.

Following the direction of the moon over the sea, he scampered along the dark woodland trail towards Pixie Cottage, now strangely named Bella Vista.

From opposite the cottage he could hear gruff voices and horses breathing heavily, but he could not see anyone. He crossed over the road and waited for whomever to come into view.

"Well, I had hold of him last night but he put up quite a fight and bolted over the heath. No doubt she'd have paid a reward if we'd nabbed him," lamented one of the guards. "No idea he was hers."

'How would they know to *whom* Davy belonged?' wondered *Magic*.

That morning, as planned, the Sheriff had called at the cottage to notify the tenant of the arrests. While there he found *Davy*'s blood-spattered medallion lying loose in the dust and informed his constables of its significance.

Davy's name was as notorious as Arabella's because they had been inseparable for over a decade and he was always with her at sea. Finding his bejewelled disc led the Sheriff to believe she had landed in England for sure.

Because the Sheriff had so many culprits to round up he could not give much thought to capturing Arabella for at least a day or two. He'd heard it was her shipwreck lying beneath the sea in smithereens and so her chances of readily escaping these shores were slim. He had no idea why she'd risked coming back or what she was up to. And she was up to quite a lot.

Chapter Seven

Risking her Life in London

Arabella stood back while the other passengers boarded the carriage, keeping her attention on the restless team of horses who would have to endure the long, fast ride pulling the coach. She handed her luggage over to the driver to be placed on the roof and was the last to climb inside. She did not smile or greet anyone else to ensure she did not have to engage in conversation or answer questions about her intended destination.

There were two horse-drawn coaches per day to London from the Spaniards Inn on the Cornish moors; she caught the later one to arrive under cover of darkness. Arabella was heading for the busy Port of London where any sailor from an overseas ship looking to claim their reward might recognise her had she not dressed as a very ladylike city dweller. There was a price on her head in many foreign lands for robbing their ships. Giving information about pirates on the 'WANTED' posters was a good way for a poor sailor to make their fortune and retire. Should there be any posters with an artist's impression of her description in the taverns she had to make her appearance unrecognisable. Being wanted, either dead or alive, gave no leeway.

Before her departure, accustomed to disguising herself on land, she'd borrowed a wide-brimmed silk hat called a bonnet to hide her face. The regulars from the inn may have wondered where she was off to. Word soon travelled and people at her destination might receive news of her before her arrival unless she was extremely cautious. Only her uncle knew of her mysterious journey but the purpose of it was still top secret, even to him.

Dressed from top-to-toe in elegant coffee-coloured silk, her fitted jacket and long swooshing dress made her feel confident; she felt she blended comfortably with her fellow travellers in their fine clothes headed for the capital. As a fearless pirate, she had always hated wearing fussy, feminine clothing. She was more at home in her practical leather britches and boots.

The carriage finally jolted away and, as it swayed from side to side on the uneven dirt road, she took a small leatherbound book from her bag and pretended to read to avoid looking at those around her. The other passengers chatted nonstop leaving her in peace to dream of her plan and to plot for any unforeseen eventualities. Just as well as she had a long, bumpy ride ahead. Arabella had no idea if she would find those she had intended to make contact with, but if her tip-offs were correct from eavesdropping on the smugglers below her garden above the beach, she had every hope they would turn up in their habitual late-night drinking places. Arabella, Queen of Pirates, very seldom failed.

The stagecoach stopped at three coaching inns to change horses and allow passengers and coachmen to get refreshments and ease their bones from the uncomfortable, unstable ride. At around eight o'clock they finally pulled into the stop in the bustling east end of London's docks. Two female passengers raised their eyebrows, looking surprised to see Arabella leaving the carriage in what appeared to be a dangerous area and not heading into the safety of the city as they were. To many observers, she gave the impression she was checking into the coaching

inn. After the carriage had pulled away and was out of sight, she strode into a maze of back streets in the misty riverside darkness to find the discreet lodgings she had been recommended.

A flickering lantern hung over the doorway casting a shadow with its amber light. She booked into a small room on the ground floor, finally free to remove her first disguise and fall onto the hard little bed for a short nap before her risky night-time escapade. Despite the guest above making the floorboards creak, she fell into a deep, refreshing sleep. She was, after all, very accustomed to creaking ships.

Arabella's next disguise was that of a man so she could enter the taverns alone without drawing attention. She tied her long blonde hair into a very tight scarf on top of her head and pulled on a fashionable men's felt hat to cover it; she had been used to doing this throughout her pirate career onboard ships. She rubbed at her eyebrows to make them look bushy and untidy and used a greyish powder on her face to give the appearance of the beginnings of a beard. Fortunately, candles dimly lit the taverns in those days and facial features were hard to make out. She had long practised making her voice sound deeper just as any actor would, depending on the part they were playing or the accent that was called for. Arabella silently lifted up the sliding casement window of her letting room and nimbly climbed out onto the cobbled stones. She pulled it down again, leaving it open an inch to be able to open it from the outside and climb back in later. It was extremely important she did all this without being heard so that no one would know or bear witness that she had been out. She wore her softest suede soled boots for the same reason. She set off for the inner docks where the noise of the late-night streets got louder and louder and she would go unnoticed amongst the hubbub. Arabella wondered how locals managed to find their way around the maze of tiny unlit passageways and back alleys in the dark without falling into the lapping inky black water of London's huge, fast-flowing river which never failed to appear mysteriously at the end of every passage, some with steep rickety wooden steps leading down to boats tied to posts. The watermen waited below for some trade, to ferry passengers to their homes on the other side. Some murky steps led to a place of execution where pirates were hung; their grisly dead bodies were left hanging high in the air for weeks, hopefully as a deterrent to warn other pirates sailing past them into the busy port.

Eventually, she reached the Black Cat Tavern, mainly from following the noise from the customers' hearty chatter and laughter. She peered through a broken pane in the stained-glass window looking for an ideal seat to head for once she got inside. She bought a pint of ale and sat in a corner facing the door to watch for anyone arriving. Hopefully someone wearing a policeman's uniform and fitting the description her uncle had given her long ago would appear, never realising his niece would store the information for a later plan. Two young constables stood close to the bar counter. Should these two men be his colleagues it would be difficult for her to strike up a casual conversation in their presence if the older officer showed up after his shift.

She sipped her ale worried she may have to return again to the inn the following night; this would put her plan for the weekend on hold by a full week – these gambling card games she hoped to gain access to only occurred late at night on Saturdays. One of the uniformed men checked his watch, commented to his companion and then both knocked back their ale in one final gulp and left. Perhaps they were still on duty and were late reporting back to the station. The constable she was waiting for may not come off his shift this side of midnight so she had to be patient.

Ten minutes later, sure enough an older man in police uniform entered and went up to the bar where he remained with his drink. She wasn't at all sure if this was the man who'd arrested her brother, Tristan. She only had a vague description from her uncle that he had thick, wavy black hair, but this person's hair was grey as a number of years had passed. This would be the perfect opportunity to go up and order another glass of ale to stand near him in case he might wander away to sit down. Arabella did not drink alcohol so ordering ale was part of an act to blend in to the surroundings without arousing suspicion. The policeman called out to the barman at the other end of the bar for a top-up, confirming all she needed to know – it *was* him – a strong Cornish accent in the heart of London. Bingo!

Now she had to tread carefully and find out where her next more important contact could be found whom she had heard moved in the same clandestine social circles with this policeman. The network of smuggling from Cornwall spread far and wide and many who received the stolen contraband goods were in London. There was a group of smugglers who apparently played cards for seriously high stakes in a private room late at night on Saturdays above an old spice warehouse. On the ground floor select customers were admitted by invitation and secret code only. In meeting up with the policeman while she was dressed as a male gave her high hopes of getting invited to play cards with this group the following evening. Her plan, though, was really a little more devious and complicated than that, if not highly dangerous.

Sure enough, as she approached the counter in the Black Cat, the policeman moved aside to allow her to order her drink and immediately struck up conversation, curious as to whom this lone young stranger in the docks could be. She lowered her voice, explaining she was in the area to join her friends for a card game which they had failed to turn up to. She was careful to avoid answering any personal questions by changing the subject as they chatted for ten minutes or so. This was how she lived her life, to stay one step ahead of whoever was pursuing her after each and every pirate raid.

To the policeman, convinced she was a young male from her clever disguise, noted she looked very young and possibly presumed his new acquaintance might be a novice and not skilled at card playing for money and so was quick to invite her, believing it would be easy to win her cash.

"If you are still in the docks tomorrow night you could come to play a round or two at the spice warehouse on Tanner Lane. I'll be there around eleven o'clock waiting at the bar. When the watchman opens the door, ask him 'Is tonight full moon?' and you will be admitted."

The man swiftly left the tavern with a sly smile on his face, seemingly pleased with himself, unaware how very pleased Arabella was with *her*self for pulling off the first part of her plan to release her younger brother from prison on the other side of the world.

The next day Arabella remained in her lodging room to avoid bumping into any of her enemies or fellow pirates who could show up in the port. She nipped out very early while the streets were empty just to buy some food to eat in her room, then she read and had a big afternoon sleep, knowing she may be out on her escapade until the early hours.

Arabella had decided to visit the spice warehouse much earlier to steer clear of the policeman who had unwittingly provided her with the address she had hoped for in her attempt to make contact with one very particular regular card player – of course she never actually intended to play cards herself. She had overheard the smugglers on the beach saying that he arrived before everyone else, let in at the rear of the premises by the night watchman.

Arabella began to get ready for her late-night encounter by putting on some long petticoats to make her fine, silk dress really stand out. She laced the bodice very tight to make her waist look smaller as society ladies did in London. Her very long hair was tucked loosely under her bonnet so her distinctive blonde locks did not give her away while walking through the busy streets of the port.

To ensure she could get away should she need to and not be tripped by the yards of silk fabric and petticoats, she packed her britches, suede boots and a thick cotton shirt into a fabric bag. Her dagger was safely accessible in an elastic garter attached to her shin.

She let herself out of the inn at around ten o'clock after the innkeeper had gone to bed and set off determinedly for the old riverside warehouse in the dock.

With her secret pass code she had no problem gaining admittance. Apparently, people from all walks of life took part in these gambling sessions, both male and female. Many were desperate to pay off a debt or to raise money quickly for a bet they had lost. Aristocrats lost their mansions this way. The gloomy ground floor was set out in discreet booths where customers could wait unseen. She sat in a booth hidden from view, right at the back near the staircase where she could listen out for the back door opening. She heard the lock clang shut, followed by muffled voices and one person's echoing footsteps ascending the stairs trailing off on the floor above her.

The barman was serving a new arrival and while engaged taking their order with his back turned, Arabella seized her opportunity. With the speed of light, she swished up the staircase in her rustling gown and composed herself outside the door of the private room where the high-stakes game was about to take place. She had no idea who would take part or turn up and, for her, this was the most dangerous aspect. Coming face to face with an old enemy was far more likely in the busy pool of the London docks. Confronting her significant contact before anyone else arrived was imperative.

Arabella entered the room to the surprise of the early startled guest, claiming she had been invited to play by the policeman who of course had not realised the night before that she was a female disguised as a man. As she had no idea what this person would look like and could not be certain of his identity, she decided to take a gamble and bluff. She presumed he was definitely who he was rumoured to be, frequenting this Saturday night gambling den, albeit incognito and in disguise himself.

"Excuse my intrusion, but I have something urgent I wish to tell you, Your Majesty," she blurted as she untied the ribbons of her silk bonnet to reveal her face, allowing her soft, golden hair to fall around her shoulders.

"Sir, I have urgent information and you will thank me for making you aware of a very dangerous situation. And for this information I require a king's pardon for my young brother wrongfully imprisoned in Australia these past two years. There is not much time; the others will soon be here."

"But… who? H-how did you..?" the king stammered nervously, totally astonished by her audacity to enter the private room knowing his exact identity and partly by her confident female beauty and the bewitching hypnotic aroma swirling his senses. He was too shocked and afraid to speak or to ask her how she knew his identity. He was alone without his guards because he liked to escape from his palace to live an ordinary existence by night

– a secret clandestine life far away from his stifling royal routine.

"I believe you are in danger, sir. Two nights ago in Half Moon Bay in the shire of Cornwall, both the magistrate and the doctor were caught red-handed by the Sheriff with a very large consignment of brandy on its way to London. They were arrested at gunpoint and taken into custody, which led to the entire smuggling gang being rounded up from their homes in the village. The name of the receiver and destination for those brandy barrels was revealed in a desperate attempt to get themselves out of the most serious trouble.

"Furthermore, the policeman who arrested my innocent brother two years ago on the moors did so unlawfully on behalf of the smugglers, of which the policeman was one, just to get my brother out of the way. He believed he'd overheard their plans for a deliberate shipwreck being discussed in the Spaniards Inn, but he had not. He was not there. He was completely innocent. The policeman, now here in London, is not so innocent and may go to great lengths to cover his own tracks and that of the entire organisation. He, too, had been moved out of the way but he has been playing card games for high stakes with you for quite some time, has he not? You must ask yourself why. He is a double-crossing traitor and provides the gang with all the information from London they need."

"What policeman?" the king demanded hesitantly.

It was obvious he had no idea which of the card players she was referring to. The policeman was hardly likely to attend these weekly gambling sessions in uniform and the king would not have known every detail of who and how the operation had been organised – unlike Arabella's carefully planned piracy schemes with tried-and-tested accomplices.

"Who on earth are you and who indeed is your brother?"

He felt very strange; not just due to the shock news of the arrests that led directly to him as having received a quota of the stolen goods, but he suddenly felt drowsy as though under a spell.

"Arabella Davy is my name and my brother is Tristan Davy. I must ask you for his pardon, sir, and an order for his release before I return to another part of the world. I intend to sail to collect my brother and we will never ever be seen again on the shores of England.

"Please send orders to your custodians in Australia to release him at once. Meanwhile, you will need to deal with your Sheriff in Cornwall before any scandal breaks regarding your involvement with the rogues he has in custody, a Dr Watts and your magistrate, Judge Julian."

The king looked pale and weak and so confused that he readily agreed to the pardon. The heady aroma of Arabella's hypnotic perfume had done its work. By the time he regained his composure to summon help to return to the palace, she would be long gone.

Arabella darted down the unlit corridor and into a dusty empty room where she pulled her britches from her fabric bag and squashed her dress and hat into it. She changed outfits without needing a mirror. She had expertly carried out this ritual of disguise many times when bidding her escape from a dangerous situation.

She heard footsteps on the stairs as she was just about to make a dash from the room that reeked of a pungent aromatic spice. The powder was scattered on the floor. She bit her bottom lip to stop herself sneezing. She remained behind the half open door wide-eyed, listening intently. For a second she heard the whoosh of the loud chattering din of customers gathered below as the internal bar door momentarily creaked open and closed again. Whoever it was had thankfully decided to return downstairs.

In her male disguise she flew down the

stairs two steps at a time, her suede soled boots making not a sound. She opened the outer rear door to the quayside and silently fled. Down on the river shore she found a huge brick and stuffed it into the bag to prevent the contents escaping and floating to the surface. She hurled the bag containing her beautiful coffee-coloured silk dress and hat into the river. She then returned in her male disguise to the Cornish village on the early morning coach where her uncle was relieved to see her back so soon… but perhaps not for long.

Chapter Eight

First Mission Accomplished

All the hours Bella had spent painting watercolours of the sea in their new clifftop garden whilst really listening to the fishermen's conversations on the beach just below, had really paid off. The many revealing conversations she overheard had painted the perfect picture with such accurate information that all had gone miraculously quickly according to her clever plan. She had gained the king's pardon for her brother's release and yet another unexpected miracle was about to fill her with happiness.

Back safely at her uncle's cottage, her heart leapt at the unexpected sight as she opened her bedroom door. *Cat Biskit Davy* was asleep on her bed. He was sleeping off the eventful night with The Secret Society for Cats in their meeting place in the underground tunnel below the house. He knew in his heart one day she would return to find him. After being washed up in a frightening shipwreck and stranded on the British Isles, he had been magically drawn to the very dwelling they would be reunited. His medallion's magic powers had not let him down even though it was now lost. In his struggle to free himself from the constable's grip, it must have fallen from his collar and he felt very upset. He had worn it since he was a kitten.

Arabella's next task was to find a ship sailing to Australia. This time she would be travelling as a cabin passenger and not in command and, therefore, *Cat Biskit Davy* could have a safe passage accompanying her on the voyage. This mission would take many weeks if not months on a sailing ship, dependent on the winds and on the number of port stops to load and unload the many mail bags and cargo.

She shut out the sunlight from the room, got undressed and climbed between the cool cotton sheets with her beloved cat already asleep snuggled on her lace pillow. He would have such a joyful surprise when he woke, having been so lonely and fretting for so long. Noticing a small cut on his neck, she gently bathed it with salt water without waking him. She whispered to him to pack his hankie on a stick with a plentiful supply of his favourite English biscuits from Mr Duff, the baker. After her exhausting London adventure and bone-rattling journey in the carriage, they slept soundly until teatime on Sunday evening.

Arabella's uncle was going to be very disappointed to hear of her imminent departure once again and so she had the best idea ever – that he should come on the voyage, too, to be reunited with his nephew, Tristan. They could all decide together where they would live even though money might be tight.

Now more than ever, following this risky experience alone, Arabella wished to give up her dangerous life as a pirate being constantly on the run. These recent events and this separation from all of them had made her realise that her family truly meant the world to her. Without sufficient money saved, her plan to go back to live in the Caribbean supporting her uncle and brother and the chief biscuit muncher himself, would not be so easy. First they must prepare to get to Australia and see what sort of shape Tristan was in after his distressing two-year ordeal. The place was renowned for hard labour. It was essential to know what he himself dreamt of should he ever be set free.

As if reading her thoughts in his dreams, *Cat Biskit Davy* stretched out his paws to gently touch her cheek, signalling all would be well. Miracle of all miracles, he appeared to be smiling for the first time.

Later that night at dinner, Arabella explained to her uncle that the voyage to rescue Tristan would include himself, if he so wished. He was excited at the prospect of seeing Tristan and all those countries on the way but felt it an impossibility without sufficient funds, especially the notion of moving to the island Arabella grew up on, which he had longed to see.

Two days later, they heard something thudding outside and awakened to find a large brandy barrel left on their doorstep. They attempted to bring it in out of sight but it was so heavy it would not budge through the front door. Arabella fetched a chisel to remove the lid because, mysteriously, it was not making the sound of a barrel containing liquid. To their astonishment the removal of the lid revealed hundreds of gleaming gold coins right up to the brim. A large fortune. Enough to retire. Enough for them all to retire. And on top of the coins was something glinting. *Davy's* lost medallion, no less.

Overnight their destiny had magically changed thanks to Arabella's bravery in saving her brother by unbelievably achieving her goal in

DAVY

personally making contact with the king himself. Her motto since childhood was that *any*thing was possible.

For the rest of her days, she would never be entirely sure if she had been rewarded by the king for giving him fair warning of the arrests that had put him in imminent danger, or that he or anyone else were merely making certain she would be able to set sail with the greatest speed to a very far off land, taking with her their secret.

The End

In the pipeline:

A planned sequel - Voyage to Australia to rescue her brother

A planned prequel - Her kidnapping from Cornwall as an infant, leading to her life of piracy

Printed in Dunstable, United Kingdom

65714604R00058